FRANK!

by Connah Brecon

RP|KIDS

PHILADELPHIA • LONDON

To the staff and students of Mt. Eliza Primary School,
who are always on time.

ISBN 978-0-7624-5423-5
Library of Congress Control Number: 2013955549

9 8 7 6 5 4 3 2 1
Digit on the right indicates the number of this printing

Designed by T. L. Bonaddio
Edited by Lisa Cheng
Typography: Special Elite, Trypewriter, and Quick End

Published by Running Press Kids
An Imprint of Running Press Book Publishers
A Member of the Perseus Books Group
2300 Chestnut Street
Philadelphia, PA 19103–4371

Visit us on the web!
www.runningpress.com/kids

Frank was late.

Frank was always late.

It wasn't that Frank was rude or unreliable.

Nor was he a dawdler or a meanderer.

UPTOWN

CRANKY KING!

REPTILE RAMPAGE!

HANDY ANDY
Watch Repair

He just liked to help out.

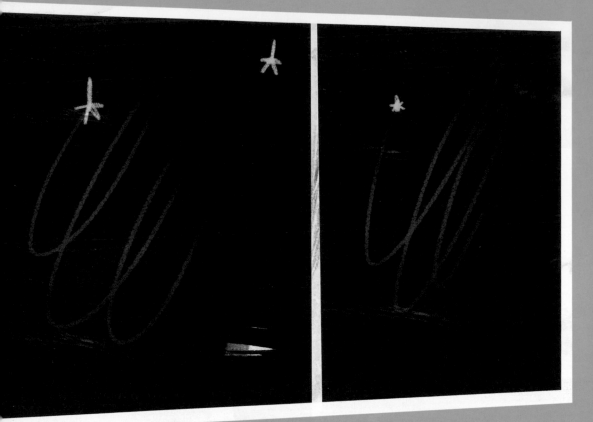

Things really began going wrong
when Frank started school.

ON THE FIRST DAY

Frank didn't arrive
until everyone had gone home.

ON THE SECOND DAY

Frank arrived
soon after lunch.

He had stopped to help
a cat stuck up a tree . . .

But the tree had become angry with Frank for climbing all over it and ran off.

It was some time
before Frank got the tree to stop.

ON THE THIRD DAY
Frank arrived
just before lunch.

Frank had been mistaken for a famous dancer
and challenged to a dance-off . . .

Which turned out surprisingly well.

ON THE FOURTH DAY

Frank arrived
at snack time.

Frank had heard a shrieking squeak
and smelled a terrible stink.

Frank had found a family of bunnies
being bullied by an ogre
and felt he needed to say something.

ERR...
EXCUSE
ME?

Which also turned out
surprisingly well...

for the bunnies.

On The Fifth Day

Frank arrived
just as the bell stopped ringing.

Frank was about to explain when . . .

EVERYTHING went dark.

THE

SCHOOL

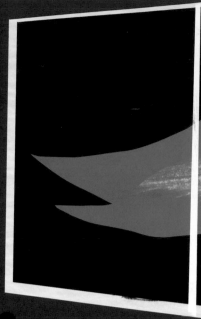

SHOOK

FROM

FLOOR

TO

ROOF.

This was NO story!

This was a

GIANT
ZOMBIE
LIZARD
KING!

The class clearly needed Frank's help.

Everyone was ready to give up
when Frank suggested . . .

HEY!

That maybe they should all
work together.

And from then on
Frank was
right on time.

HERALD NEWS

TOWN HIT
BY
TONE-DEAF
VAMPIRE
KITTENS